D0056319

Courageous Adventures of

The Konscious Kidz

THE NEIGHBORHOOD

This book is dedicated to Celeste Renee, Simone Isabella, and Vivienne Rose. Your lives have changed our lives. You inspire us to become the best versions of ourselves. You are pure love and light, stay conscious.

Courageous Adventures of

The Konscious Kidz

THE NEIGHBORHOOD

John Casselberry
and Madeline Connor

ILLUSTRATION BY JERL LAWS

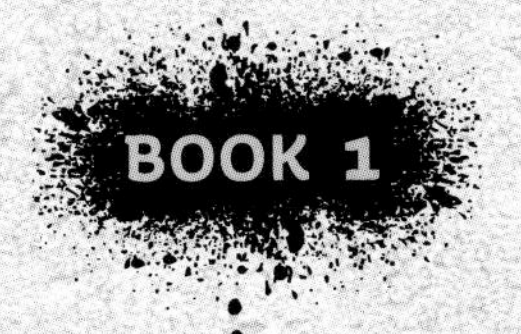

ISBN 978-1-7339836-0-0 (Hardcover)

Library of Congress Control Number: 2019906809
Any references to historical events, real people, or real places are used fictitiously. Names, characters, and places are products of the author's imagination.

For information about discounts on bulk purchases, educational copies, or sales promotions, please contact Free Planet Press sales department at www.freeplanetpress.com.

Illustrations and cover art by Jerl Laws
Book design by Barbara Genetin

Printed in the United States of America.
First printing edition 2019

10 9 8 7 6 5 4 3 2 1

free planet press

www.freeplanetpress.com

CONTENTS

Meet the Konscious Kidz

Six neighborhood friends from different backgrounds who play, laugh, and grow together. They face the many different challenges and adventures of life as a community, showing us that we are all more alike than we are different.

FLACO is Puerto Rican. He loves music and dancing and also has a green thumb like his grandmother. Flaco gravitates to the natural sciences; nutrition and health are his passion. Flaco moved to the Konscious Kidz's neighborhood from Brooklyn.

BELLE is African American; she is a natural athlete and a gifted writer, who has dreams of becoming a rock star/drummer. Belle is an advocate for social justice and strives for things being fair and equitable. She doesn't hesitate to step up to a cause and rally the Konscious Kidz around a mission for seeking justice in any given situation.

LYRIC is Irish American. He is the new kid on the block. He more recently moved to the neighborhood from a Midwestern suburb of Detroit. He inherited the gift of the spoken word from his grandfather. Lyric is a poet, a deep thinker, and a philosopher with a streak of court jester.

V-GIRL is Belle's fraternal twin sister, a nurturer who exudes love and compassion. She is an artist, dancer, and a keen observer of life. V-Girl is passionate about nature, ecology, and the ecosystem. She wants everything to be in harmony and balance.

PIXEL is Asian; his father is Korean American and his mother is from Thailand. He is gentle, yet strong; a peaceful warrior. He has an unsuspecting sense of humor. He is a tech savvy optimist with a passion for music production. He is always positive and solution-oriented.

IVY is Native American, with Navajo and Cherokee heritage. She was born on her family's ranch in New Mexico, and moved to the neighborhood with her mom one year ago when her parents separated. Ivy is confident and outspoken, especially for her age. She is grounded and in tune with herself and the world around her. One of her passions is animal welfare, which explains why she's a vegan!

"GUARDIAN ANGEL"
Mural by Chris Granillo

1

Stand by Me

One fine day, in the middle of town, on their favorite street, with their favorite friends, at Gio's, the Konscious Kidz were enjoying their favorite pizza. It was cheese—extra cheese—with zucchini and tomatoes.

They always met at Gio's when they wanted to plan their next courageous adventure.

"I sure do love eating pizza!" said Flaco.

"You just love *eating*!" teased Lyric.

"That's true," giggled Flaco, "but I really love eating *pizza*."

"Hey, do you want to go over to the Community

Center to see if those kids are doing another dance-off?“ said V-Girl. She loved dancing, all kinds of dancing.

“We went last Saturday,” Pixel replied, “and I’m not so good at dancing. I felt like everybody was laughing at me.”

“Well, maybe not everybody . . . ” giggled Lyric.

“No one was laughing at you,” said Ivy. “They were just having fun dancing.”

“Well, I felt silly,” said Pixel.

“Bro! You might have felt silly, but I saw you do some pretty funky moves out there!” said Lyric.

“Hey, Lyric! You didn’t do so bad either!” laughed Belle. “And it sure was fun!”

“Yeah!” They all laughed and agreed.

“So what are we gonna do today?” asked Belle.

"We could go to the skatepark," Ivy chimed in.

"YEAH!" they all cheered.

"Ooh, yay!" squealed Belle. "I love skateboarding!"

"We know," smiled Lyric.

So they finished their pizza, and off they went.

"See ya later, Gio! Thanks for the pizza!"

"Bye, kids, have fun today," said Gio, "and remember, what do I always say?"

"Be safe!" they all shouted back.

When they arrived at the park, there were a lot of people there. It just so happened that there was going to be a big contest this weekend, and it seemed like the whole town had come to watch. There was even a crew from the local news channel.

"Wow, everyone, look! Isn't that Jimmy 'Wheels' Bozzini, the famous skateboarder?" exclaimed Belle.

"I don't know," said Lyric, "but I'm gonna get on TV when they see how good I can skate!"

So they all took off in different directions on their skateboards. It wasn't long after that when Ivy

noticed Pixel had stopped skating and was sitting alone, looking quite sad, almost like he was going to cry.

"Hey, what's the matter?" Ivy asked as she sat down next to him.

"I have to leave, but I wanna stay," said Pixel.

"What do you mean? Why do you have to leave? We just got here!" pleaded Ivy.

"Those boys are making fun of me 'cause I'm not very good," Pixel said sadly, "and that big kid said I shouldn't even try because I'm so bad. He told me I have to leave because I'm just in everybody's way."

Just then Belle came over. "What's going on?"

"Pixel is really sad because those kids are making fun of him and that one is trying to bully him into leaving," explained Ivy, pointing.

"Wait here . . . " said Belle.

Belle took off and headed straight for the bullies.

"What do you think she's saying to them?" asked Pixel. "They are so much bigger than her!"

They could see Belle fearlessly standing there talking to the biggest kid while all of his friends stood around Belle, looking pretty tough.

Then, the group of kids all started to laugh at her, but she just calmly stood there and continued to talk to the bully who was picking on her friend. Soon she stuck her hand out; they shook, and Belle headed back over with an interesting look on her face.

"What happened . . . what did you say to those kids?" asked Pixel "Do I have to leave . . . ?"

"Nope, you don't have to leave; they will!" said Belle.

"What?! How'd you do that?!" Pixel and Ivy both wanted to know.

"Well . . . first we have to do something" said Belle.

"I knew it was too good to be true," interrupted Pixel.

"Now hold on, Pixel, it's simple: we're gonna meet back here next Saturday to have a skate-off. The loser has to stay away from the park for two weeks."

"Are you kidding me?!" cried Pixel. "I can't win against those guys! I can barely skate."

"Don't worry, I didn't tell them you were gonna skate. I only said if 'we' win they have to leave for two weeks."

Then Ivy said, "Yeah, but Belle, even though you are a really good skater, your board is pretty old and not very fast."

"Well . . . I figured since Pixel is so good at fixing things, he could help me make my board better and faster," winked Belle. "Then I'll challenge the bully and we'll have a pretty good chance of winning. Besides, he doesn't even know I can skate."

"Oh, boy! He is in for a real surprise!" chirped Lyric.

As soon as they got back to their neighborhood, Pixel and Belle went to Pixel's house.

"Hey, Dad, can we go in your workshop?" asked Pixel.

"What are you two up to?" replied Pixel's dad.

"We want to fix Belle's skateboard," said Pixel.

"As long as you clean up after yourselves and put everything back when you finish," said his dad.

"We will, we promise," said Belle.

Then Pixel and Belle went to work fixing Belle's skateboard. Pixel started by checking her board to see what it needed.

"Hey, Belle, your wheels barely spin. It looks like the bearings are pretty old and actually kinda rusty," said Pixel.

"Yeah, I know," said Belle. "I just never replaced them 'cause it seemed to be working enough for me to still have fun on."

Soon the rest of the crew showed up, curious and excited. V-Girl danced and did pirouettes, giggling with anticipation.

"Hey, how's it going everybody?" asked Flaco.

"Hey, Flaco," replied Belle, "we're figuring it out now."

"Well," said Pixel, "I think all we really need to do is put on some new wheels and stiffer trucks to make it more stable when you skate."

"That sounds great, but how much is all of that going to cost?" asked Belle.

Just then Pixel's dad walked in. "How much is what going to cost?"

"Belle and Pixel are fixing her skateboard so she can race the bullies," said Lyric.

"What bullies?!" asked Dad.

"The ones at the park today," Lyric answered.

"They tried to make Pixel leave, but Belle challenged them to a skate competition for rights to the park for two weeks!"

"Hmm," Pixel's dad pondered for a moment. "I see. I think I'll come and watch this competition, just to make sure everyone plays fair."

"Yeah," said Flaco, "because they don't exactly seem like the kind of kids that play by the rules."

"Dad, if we gave you the money, would you order these parts for us online?" Pixel asked.

"You know what, you kids keep your money. I want to pay for your parts Belle, for being an ally to Pixel," his dad said.

"Thanks, but you don't need to do that. It's my board, and Pixel's already helping me by figuring out what it needs."

"Yeah, but you stood up to those bullies for me! And now you're taking a chance of not even being able to go to the park for two weeks if we don't win," explained Pixel. "I think you should accept my dad's offer."

"OK, I will. Thank you, Mr. Hahn," Belle agreed. "It is going to be great to out-skate them 'cause they were being so mean."

"You know, Belle, I think that bully just needs somebody to love him," V-Girl chimed in.

"My abuelita always says that hurt people, *hurt* people," Flaco said. "I guess that's what she means."

"Your abuela is right," Pixel's dad replied, "but we are all still responsible for how we treat each other, and I want to make sure you kids are not mistreated."

The next Saturday finally came. When the Konscious Kidz arrived at the park, the bully and his friends were already there practicing.

"Wow, Belle, those guys are pretty good!" said Lyric.

Belle and Pixel just smiled.

"Do you really think you can beat them?" Flaco wondered aloud.

"I believe in you Belle!" said V-Girl.

Ivy agreed. "Yeah, Belle, you can do it! We're all behind you."

Just then, the bully came over. "You guys ready? I didn't even think you were gonna show up," he taunted.

"Yeah, we're ready," said Belle. "How about if we race twice around the park and do two tricks each?"

"I'll video it on my phone so we can watch the

FINISH

MAKE SKATE GREAT
Eat more veggies

footage and decide," Pixel's dad assured them.

"And I have my camera too!"said V-Girl.

"We can video it on our phones," said Ivy.

"OK . . . " said the bully. "GO!" And he took off.

Belle, surprised, jumped on her board and took off after him. He was so busy laughing and gloating about fooling her that he missed a turn and fell into the grass. Before he could get back up, Belle caught up and they were side by side. The bully did his first trick on one of the ramps. It was a caballerial, a 360 degree fakie. Belle did one too, but added a kickflip.

"OOOOH!" everyone shouted.

"Go Belle!" shouted V-Girl.

The bully, not to be outdone, then did a rail slide, goofy foot. So Belle did a nose slide right behind him. They both headed for the finish line. By now a crowd was gathering, and more people pulled out their phones and started to record the race. Up one ramp and down another, Belle pushed her board as fast as she could. The new wheels Pixel put on were spinning faster and faster. When they crossed the finish line, it was really close. Everybody waited to see the playback to determine who won.

They all watched the different videos together, and after a few minutes, they all had to agree that Belle was the first to cross the finish line.

The bully's friends looked disappointed. Surprised, they asked him, "So what are you gonna do? We're not gonna let these kids have the park for two weeks, are we?!"

Without saying a word, he turned from his friends and walked over to the Konscious Kidz.

"Congratulations, you won fair and square! I never would have expected you to be so good. I guess a deal is a deal, so we will stay away for two weeks."

"Wait a minute," said Ivy.

The Kidz huddled up, and after some discussion, V-Girl made the announcement.

"We all voted, and we would rather us all be friends than have you guys not have fun here too."

The bully and his friends all looked surprised again.

"Wow," said the bully, "I guess I had you kids all wrong. You guys are really cool!"

Lyric stepped up first. "That's OK, we knew we were cool! My name's Lyric!"

"My name's Logan," their new friend laughed, "and these are my buddies." Then Logan looked at Belle and asked, "What I want to know is, how did you get your skateboard to go so fast?!"

Belle pointed to Pixel and said, "He did it, he can fix anything!"

Then Logan asked, "So, Pixel, you think you could show me how to make my board go faster too?"

"Sure," said Pixel, "just bring—"

"Wait a minute," interrupted Belle. "Logan, I think

you owe Pixel an apology first. Then how about you teach him some skate tricks?"

"Hahaha, you got a deal!" laughed Logan. "She's right, Pixel. I'm sorry I was being a jerk."

"Hey, Logan, you were being a jerk but I'll forgive you, too, if you show me how to do a fakie!" Lyric blurted out.

"Sure, Lyric!" Logan chuckled. "You can help me teach Pixel while we're at it." As the three of them headed towards the ramps, Pixel was beaming.

It seemed that everybody knew something somebody else could learn from, and that's what makes having friends so cool!

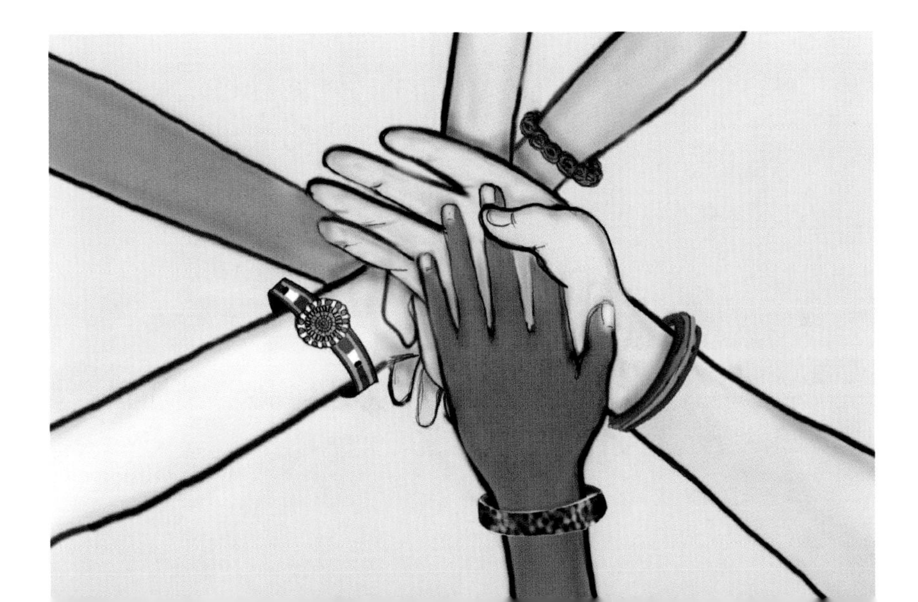

“BORN TO BE LOVED”

Mural by Chris “Royyal Dog” Shim

3
VON

2

Save Gio's

It was another lovely day. Ivy and Lyric were on their way to meet their friends at Gio's Pizza Shop to plan their next courageous adventure.

Just as they turned the corner to Gio's, Flaco came running up to them. He was quite upset.

Ivy took one look at him and asked, "Flaco, what's wrong?!"

"It's the worst thing EVER!" said Flaco.

"What is . . . ?" asked Lyric.

"The shop . . . Gio's Pizza Shop . . . " stammered Flaco, barely able to speak.

"What happened to Gio's?" Ivy wanted to know.

"C'mon!" he said, as he turned and ran.

They followed him down the street and around the corner, where they found the rest of their friends standing in front of the pizza shop.

"What's going on?" asked Lyric.

"Look," said Belle, "Gio's Pizza Shop is closing for good!"

Just then, Gio came walking up.

"Gio! What's going on?!" asked Flaco.

"Hi, kids. Come on in," said Gio.

They all followed him into the shop and gathered around anxiously to find out what was going on.

"Well, everybody, you know the big new pizza place downtown? It is able to sell pizzas for less than I do," Gio explained. "A lot of my customers are going there now. I'm not getting enough business to stay open."

"But Gio, you can't close! We all love your pizza and we all love you!" said V-Girl.

"Hey, Gio, what if you made special pizzas that they don't have?" suggested Pixel.

"Yeah, Gio, who says you have to stick to the same as everybody else?" said Flaco.

"I'm sorry, kids, but different ingredients would cost even more, and with business as slow as it is, I can't afford it," said Gio.

"Hey, Flaco, why don't you tell Gio what we were talking about yesterday?" said V-Girl.

"Well," started Flaco, "we were talking about how good the veggies from my garden taste, and wondering why more people don't grow their own instead of buying from the big companies."

"Well, kids, I guess a lot of people think it's easier to just buy them," said Gio.

"Hey, Gio, what if you made pizzas with fresh organic veggies like Flaco grows?" asked Belle.

"Yeah, Gio. If we go get some for you, would you make us one?" asked Flaco.

"Sure, kids, but that's not going to be enough for me to stay in—"

Before he could finish, they were all out of the door and running to Flaco's garden. After a short while, they were back with a wagon full of fresh tomatoes, zucchinis, peppers, carrots, radishes, and even some basil and herbs.

GIO'S

"WOW!" said Gio. "You mean you got all of this from your garden, Flaco?"

"Yeah, my grandma taught me how to grow veggies!"

So Gio took some of the fresh vegetables and made the kids two extra large special pizzas. They were so good that V-Girl and Flaco decided to cut them into small pieces and offer samples to people walking past the shop. Before long, there was a line of people trying to order some of Gio's fresh veggie pizzas. Gio was making them as fast as he could, until he was all sold out.

"Gio, what if we plant a big garden out back?" suggested Lyric. "Maybe we could get our folks to help us haul away all the stuff you have back there and turn it into a garden!"

"That sounds great, Lyric, but it would be a lot of work and it would be months before we even produced any vegetables," said Gio.

"Yeah, but it would be fun," said Pixel. "Besides, what have you got to lose?"

"Hmm . . . Well, if you kids really feel like you want to, I actually love the idea," said Gio.

So for the next few days the Kidz showed up at the shop with rakes and shovels and started clearing out the weeds and trash. They filled barrels and garbage bags.

Then, one morning, as some of the kids showed up to continue working on cleaning the yard, there were at least a dozen people standing outside the shop, waiting for them. There was Mr. Brown, the garbageman, who brought his truck. Mrs. Lee was there with her construction tools. Mr. Jameson was there from the nursery with his wheelbarrow and gardening tools. Pixel's parents were there; in fact, to their surprise all of the Kidz's parents were there. Standing smack in the middle was Pixel, with a big grin on his face.

"Pixel, what's going on? We were wondering where you were. Where did all these people come from?" asked Ivy.

"I posted an online campaign and word got around. You should see how many hits we're getting! People are even pledging to donate more time and supplies to the 'Save Gio's Pizza Campaign,'" said Pixel. "Isn't it awesome?!"

"Is that why V-Girl's been taking so many pictures?" asked Gio.

"Yep," grinned Pixel. "People see how much we're doing on our own, and they want to support us."

"Wow, you kids really seem to know what you're doing!" exclaimed Gio.

"Not really," chuckled V-Girl. "We just believe in why we're doing it, so we trust it to work out!"

So as the kids would dig out weeds and turn the soil, the adults loaded the debris and hauled it away. After that, they planted all kinds of vegetables. They planted tomatoes, carrots, zucchinis, onions, squash, broccoli, and even spinach.

Every day, the Kidz took turns watering the plants and making sure no weeds grew. They put up wire frames to help the tomatoes, and added plant food to the water to make the plants strong and healthy. Finally, after eight long weeks most of the veggies were ready for harvest.

Of course, V-Girl was taking pictures every step of the way, which Pixel posted to the online page they had started.

By harvest time, there were many people following "The Save Gio's Pizza Campaign." Even people from neighboring towns! Gio decided it was a good time to expand the size of the dining area, and also opened up the patio for seating.

Finally, Gio's was ready for the big day—the day they had all been waiting for: the opening of the new patio garden.

They put up flyers and posters all over town, and Pixel posted about it online.

People came from all over. They were lined up outside, eager for Gio to open the doors. There was a salsa band playing on the patio, and Gio was making pizzas as fast as he could to keep up with the crowd's orders. Pixel was at the door welcoming everybody, Ivy and Lyric were showing folks to their seats, and Flaco was taking orders and suggesting different veggie combinations to people.

Everyone was so excited. The Konscious Kidz were the happiest of all as they sat down to an extra-extra-large Gio's Veggie Special that Gio made just for them.

Torani

Free
Humanity

"LOVE YOUR CITY"
Mural by Free Humanity
Unity

3

Cocomo

It was Saturday!

V-Girl and Belle woke up really excited! Saturday was their favorite day! This Saturday was different though; it was special. This Saturday was the day they were going to the animal shelter to pick out a brand new puppy!

"I can't wait!" V-Girl told Belle.

"Me, neither!" said Belle. "What do you think he'll look like?"

"Maybe it'll be a girl puppy," said V-Girl.

"I don't care, I just know that I love puppies!" giggled Belle.

"Me too!" said V-Girl.

"Girls, let's go, get dressed. Dad's already in the car waiting for us," their mom called out.

They rushed to get dressed. This was one time Mom didn't have to tell them more than once to get ready! They brushed their teeth, picked out clothes, and got dressed so fast that when V-Girl looked up, she had to laugh.

"What's so funny?" asked Belle.

"Look," pointed V-Girl, "you put your shirt on inside out."

"Oops," laughed Belle as she turned it around. Once they were dressed, they both ran downstairs. They were so excited they were barely able to eat their oatmeal.

"C'mon, Mom, let's go," said Belle, as she headed to the door.

So they all climbed in the car and off they went. The animal rescue shelter was just downtown, so it didn't take long to get there; but to the girls, it may as well have been a thousand miles away.

Once they arrived, they all went to the front desk to see Dr. Robinson, the veterinarian who ran the rescue shelter.

"Hi, Dr. Robinson!" chirped V-Girl.

"Hi, girls. What brings you down here?" answered Dr. Robinson, pretending she didn't remember.

"We're getting a puppy today!" they squealed.

"A puppy, are you sure that's today?" she teased.

"Yes!" They knew she was teasing; Dr. Robinson was always happy to see the girls. Sometimes she would let them come down and help out with feeding some of the animals and walking the smaller dogs.

"Well, then. I guess we better go and see who we have in the back today—that is, if you're sure."

"We're sure!" the girls said in unison.

They all walked to the back where the kennels were, and no sooner had they got back there than V-Girl spotted Cocomo, a little Jack Russell Terrier.

"Oh, he's so cute," she said. "When did he get here?"

"Just this week," said Dr. Robinson, looking at her clipboard.

"Oh, can he come home with us?" Belle asked her parents.

"I don't see why not," said Dad. "What do you say, Doc?"

"He has all of his shots," said Dr Robinson. "You just need to fill out some forms, and he's all yours."

"OK, girls, but first, do you both remember what you promised?" asked Mom.

"Yes, Mom!" they said. "We will take such good care of him!"

The girls couldn't wait to call the rest of their friends as soon as they got home so everybody could meet Cocomo, the new puppy. All their friends came right over: Ivy, Lyric, Pixel, and Flaco.

Pixel brought a chew toy for Cocomo. Flaco brought some doggie treats. Ivy and Lyric brought him a nice pillow to sleep on for his first night in a new home.

They were all so excited to meet him. They played and took turns throwing a ball for him. After a while, they all went down to play by the creek and cool off in the water. Cocomo jumped right in with everybody else. By the time they got back home, all the kids were covered in mud and Cocomo was so dirty, you couldn't even tell what color he was.

When Mom saw them coming up the walkway to the house, she stopped them right in their tracks.

"Whoa! Wait just a minute. You are not coming in this house like that!" she said. "Take off those muddy shoes at the door and you girls get in the bathtub."

"Hey, Mom, Cocomo needs a bath too," said Belle. "Can he get in the tub with us?"

"I have a better idea," said Mom. "How about all of you kids go to the backyard, and we'll wash all of you with the garden hose? You can give Cocomo his first bath together. I'll get you some towels."

"Yeah, that sounds like fun, Mom!" said V-Girl.

"Arf!' said Cocomo, wagging his little tail.

The next day, Mom went into the girls' room to get them up for breakfast, but V-Girl wasn't in her bed.

"Belle, where's your sister?"

"I don't know." answered Belle, yawning and rubbing her eyes.

They looked everywhere for V-Girl—well, almost everywhere.

"Mom, here she is!" said Belle.

There she was, sound asleep, curled up next to Cocomo on his big pillow that Ivy and Lyric had brought.

"V-Girl, what are you doing sleeping on the floor?" asked Mom.

"I didn't want Cocomo to be all alone on his first night here. So I came to sit with him until he fell asleep, but I guess we both fell asleep." She grinned.

"Well, come get some breakfast. What are you two up to today?"

"Our friends are coming over and we're gonna play with Cocomo and teach him some tricks. Maybe he can be a famous dog!" said Belle.

"Maybe . . . " Mom smiled.

After the girls had their breakfast and washed up, they got dressed, brushed their teeth, and went out in the front yard to wait for their friends to arrive. Ivy and Lyric got there first. Pixel and Flaco came down the street on their bicycles. They all took turns trying to teach Cocomo things like "sit," "lay down," and "fetch the ball." He was everybody's new best friend, and they all loved little Cocomo.

Just then Dad came out.

"Hi, kids, how's our new little friend doing?"

"He's awesome, Dad," said V-Girl. "We're teaching him how to sit, wanna see?"

"That's great!" said Dad. "Just remember to be gentle with him because he is still getting used to being here."

"OK, Dad." Belle promised.

"Hey, everybody, did you hear that?" said Flaco. "It's the ice cream truck!"

Sure enough, everyone did hear it: the familiar jingle playing from the ice cream truck. In fact, they could see it turning the corner and coming down the street.

"Let's go, you guys!" said Lyric, as he ran out of the gate.

Everybody chased after him except V-Girl. She stopped to put Cocomo's leash and collar on before running after her friends.

"I'm going to get a strawberry ice cream cone," announced Ivy.

"You always get strawberry," laughed Pixel. "I want chocolate!"

"I know, I love strawberry! It's my favorite." Ivy smiled.

All the kids from the neighborhood came out when they heard the truck. They were all crowding around, wanting to be first in line.

Cocomo wasn't used to so many strangers. The boys with the skateboards who came riding up made him nervous. Since his collar was new, he could still wiggle his little head right out of it. He decided it would be best if he just went back to the yard and waited for the Kidz.

V-Girl was so busy thinking about what kind of ice cream she was going to get that she didn't notice Cocomo had slipped out of his collar and went running down the street to get back home. The problem was, he was going the wrong way!

STOP

Ivy noticed first. “V-Girl! Where’s Cocomo?!”

“Oh my gosh!” exclaimed V-Girl as she looked down.

Sure enough, he was gone!

V-Girl dropped her ice cream and turned, running back to the yard, hoping he went back there!

“Cocomo . . . Cocomo, where are you? Come here, boy!” she called out.

Everybody came running up behind her. “Is he here?” asked Pixel.

“No!” cried V-Girl. “This is terrible! Where is he?! Mom, Dad, Cocomo’s gone! We can’t find him! Daddy!”

“I’ll get them,” Belle said as she ran to get their parents.

Belle and Dad come running out of the house. V-Girl was sobbing so hard she could barely stand. Dad scooped her up and hugged her.

“Where did you see him last?” asked Dad.

“I had him on the leash, like you said. But I guess I wasn’t paying attention, ’cause when I looked down, he was gone!" sobbed V-Girl. "Oh, Daddy, please help! We've got to find him! He's all alone, and if something happens to him I'll never forgive myself!"

"We'll find him. I'll get my keys and drive around the neighborhood. I'll ask Mom to stay here in case he comes back."

"I'll stay here with V-Girl," said Belle.

"No, I can't stay here," said V-Girl as she jumped to her feet, "we need to find him! He's lost and all alone!"

"OK, everybody," directed Lyric. "Let's split up and go look in different directions. If we hurry he shouldn't be far!"

"Don't worry, V-Girl, we'll find him!" said Pixel.

"Yeah, he'll be OK. He's so smart, he'll probably find his way home before you know it," said Ivy.

"Let's all meet back here in one hour," said Lyric, "in case he does come back."

Pixel and Flaco jumped on their bikes and took off in separate directions. Ivy went towards Main St. and Lyric headed towards the creek. V-Girl and Belle went to look over by the playground. Belle decided she was going to stick close to V-Girl because she was so upset. Belle didn't want her sister to have to be alone right now.

They looked by the swings. They looked at Gio's. They looked by the school. They looked in Flaco's garden. They even looked in Mr. Jameson's chicken coop. After searching for an hour, they all headed back to V-Girl and Belle's house. Mom was on the phone calling the shelters in town to see if anybody had found Cocomo, and leaving the home phone number in case he showed up.

Dad pulled into the driveway. V-Girl was so sad; her new best friend was lost, and she felt like it was all her fault.

"Oh, why didn't I just leave him in the yard? If only I didn't go get ice cream. Oh, Cocomo, where are you? I'm so sorry."

"Hey, it's not over. We just started looking," Lyric assured her.

Pixel chimed in. “I’m going to go home to make some flyers. Belle, can you text me some of the pictures you took of him yesterday?”

“My dad is going to be doing his community route today. I’ll ask him to keep an eye out also,” offered Flaco.

“I’ll go with you, Pixel, to help make the flyers,” said Ivy, “and my mom can make copies for us.”

So they all set out on a mission to find their missing friend Cocomo. For the next few days, they put up flyers all over town and checked animal shelters, hoping somebody had found him.

“Hey, you guys. Thanks for trying so hard to help find Cocomo, but I guess he’s really gone,” said V-Girl.

“He’s not gone, V-Girl,” said Ivy. “We just don’t know where he is. It’s all gonna be OK, you’ll see.”

“How will I ever face Dr. Robinson again? She trusted me.”

“She still trusts you,” replied Ivy. “It was an accident, it could have happened to any of us.”

"Well, I think I should go apologize for not taking better care of him."

So they headed over to the animal shelter where Dr. Robinson worked. As they walked in, she was at the front desk on the phone. She looked up, smiled like she always did, and hung up the phone.

"Hi, Kidz! V-Girl! I was just calling your house. Come with me, I have something to show you."

"But, Dr. Robinson, I have something I need to say . . . "

"OK, but first come with me," insisted Dr. Robinson.

"Dr. Robinson, I lost him, I lost Cocomo! I'm so sorry! I know you trusted me and I promised to take care of him, but now he's gone and it's all my fault!" V-Girl blurted out as she burst into tears. "Will you ever forgive me?"

“Oh, V-Girl, it’s OK, honey,” Dr. Robinson said. “Come with me, dear.”

So they all followed her into the back, and when they turned the corner they couldn’t believe their eyes! Sitting there, wagging his little tail, was Cocomo!

“Cocomo!” shrieked V-Girl. “Oh my gosh, where have you been?! Oh, thank you, Dr. Robinson! How did you find him?”

“I didn’t. When I came back from lunch a few minutes ago, he was sitting at the front door!”

“Oh, Cocomo! I am never going to lose you again!” promised V-Girl.

“Arf! Arf!” answered Cocomo in agreement.

So they all took him home and played in the sprinklers to celebrate. Everybody was so happy to have their little friend back.

JUSTICE

"THE RED ROAD"
Mural by Jason Dobbs,
Intertribal Friendship House

4

Let's Talk

DING DONG!

"Ivy, can you answer the door?" said Mom. "It's probably Lyric. He always seems to know when we're making cookies."

"Sure, Mom."

Sure enough it was Lyric, Ivy's buddy.

"Hey, Ivy, what's up? Whoa, do I smell cookies?" he asked as his face lit up.

"Yeah, Mom's making them for the Halloween party. Come on in."

"Hi, Lyric," said Mom from the kitchen. "You're just in time for testing the first batch."

"Well, only if I have to . . . " he laughed.

"No thanks, Mom. I don't want any," said Ivy.

"Whaaat?!" said Lyric, not believing what he heard. "Are you sick or something? You love your mom's cookies as much as I do!"

"OK, dear. Well, I'll just put a few here in case you change your mind," said Mom. Mom put a few cookies on a plate for the two friends and poured them some milk.

"Thanks, Ms. Ramirez," said Lyric.

He took the tray with the milk and cookies, and followed Ivy out to the backyard.

"Your mom makes, like, the best cookies ever! I think if I lived here, I'd turn into a cookie!" he said as he devoured one cookie after another.

"Yeah, they're alright," said Ivy.

"Hey, are you kidding me? 'Alright?' They're amazing!" he said as he guzzled down the milk and plopped down on the grass next to his friend.

Ivy just sat there staring off like he wasn't there.

"OK, what's going on? Don't try to tell me nothing either. I've seen that face before. Is it your dad?" Lyric wanted to know.

"It's not just my dad," Ivy burst out, fighting back tears. "Why can't they just say sorry for whatever happened and make up?! I'm so mad at them both. Can't they see what this is doing to me—to us all?!"

"Hey, look at the bright side," said Lyric, "you get to spend summer vacations with your dad."

"It's not the same! We used to have family vacations together. I just want my family back," Ivy said. "You have your parents."

"I'm sorry, Ivy. It's not fair. I wish I could help," said Lyric. "Grown-ups just don't make sense to me sometimes. Well, actually, most of the time. Besides, just because my parents live in the same house doesn't mean I have it better than you. They're gone, like, all the time. At least your parents pay attention to you when you see them."

"I know," said Ivy, "they're actually really good to

me. I don't mean to sound like I don't appreciate all that they do. I . . . I just . . . I don't know, it's hard to explain. I love being with my dad, but when I'm there, I miss my mom and you and all the rest of our friends. Then, when I'm here, I miss my dad and my friends there."

"You know what I just thought of?" Lyric quipped. "You don't have less, you have more."

"More? How do you figure that?"

"Yeah, 'cause you have friends and family here and at your dad's," he said.

"Hey, Lyric, I know you're trying to make me feel better," Ivy said, "but right now I'm just really sad about it and don't know what to do about it."

"I know," Lyric said. "I'm sorry you're sad. Whaddya say we go find the rest of the kids and get your mind off of this for a minute?"

"OK, sure. I think I'd like that."

So off they went. They decided to head over to the twins' house to see if they wanted to come out and play. When they got there, Pixel was in the front yard playing with Cocomo, the twins' dog.

"Hey, Pixel!" they both said, almost in harmony.

"Hey, you two!" he answered. "Where are you guys coming from?"

"We were at Ivy's house. Her mom is making cookies for the school Halloween party," Lyric said, grinning. "I was the official taste tester."

"Oh man!" Pixel said. "I LOVE your mom's cookies, Ivy, I wish I knew! I would have been there in a flash!"

"Don't worry, Pixel," said Ivy, "we left before 'Cookie Monster' here could eat all of them."

"Yeah, I sure would have tried," laughed Lyric. "Hey, where's V-Girl and Belle?"

"They'll be out in a minute," replied Pixel. "Their dad said they have to finish their morning chores. Whaddya guys wanna do today?"

"I think we should make up some costumes for the Halloween party," said Lyric. "Besides, we need to cheer up our buddy. She's a little sad today," he whispered into Pixel's ear.

Pixel nodded in agreement. "OK! Let's go down to the thrift store when V-Girl and Belle come out, they're great at making up costumes! Last year they made you the coolest mummy ever, Lyric! What do you think, Ivy, you wanna?"

"Yeah, sure," said Ivy. "That sounds like fun. I could use some laughs today."

"Great! Here they come now!" said Lyric. "Hey, Belle! Hey, V-Girl! We wanna go to the thrift store and pick out some stuff to make Halloween costumes. You guys down for that?"

"Oh, definitely," said V-Girl. "That's only, like, one of my all-time favorite things to do!"

"Yay! Dress up!" exclaimed Belle. "Let's go!"

So they headed down to the store, and on the way there they stopped by Flaco's house to see if he wanted to join them. Flaco came out munching on a large tripleta sandwich. The tripleta is Puerto Rico's answer to the Cuban sandwich. It combines chicken, ham, and beef.

"Wow, Flaco!" laughed Lyric. "That sandwich is as big as your head, dude!"

"Yeah," Flaco replied, "but the best part is it's a nacho sandwich!"

"Huh? A nacho sandwich?" said Lyric, puzzled.

"Uh-huh, it's 'not your' sandwich!" laughed Flaco.

"Oh," said Lyric. "I see you're full of jokes today. You got me with that one. Hey, we're going to the thrift store to get stuff for Halloween costumes. Wanna come with us?"

"Sure," said Flaco. "What are you gonna be this year?"

"I don't know, I'm hoping V-Girl or Belle can help me come up with a cool idea," Lyric answered.

"Hey, Lyric! I know! You and Ivy can be Sonny and Cher!" Pixel piped in.

"Who?" asked Belle.

"Sonny and Cher. My mom used to listen to them back in the olden days. She has records in the garage. When we get back, I'll show you."

"Um, OK, maybe," said Lyric. "What do you think, Ivy? Ever heard of them?"

"I don't know, maybe. I'm going to go home, you guys, I don't feel like doing this right now," Ivy said.

"Huh? What happened?" asked Flaco, puzzled.

Lyric pulled Flaco aside and told him why Ivy was so sad.

In that moment, Flaco knew he had to help her. He didn't know what he was going to say or how he would help, but he knew he had to try.

"Hey, Ivy, wait up!" said Flaco. "I'm gonna go back that way. I'll walk with you."

"Um . . . OK," said Ivy.

As they walked back, Flaco decided to share something with Ivy that he hadn't really talked about with the other kids.

"I'm sorry you're not feeling well, Ivy," Flaco said.

"I'm just upset about my parents," said Ivy. "I'll be OK I guess."

"You know, you're right. You will be OK. It is still OK to feel sad when you miss someone, though," he said. "I miss my mom a lot still."

"Where is your mom?" asked Ivy. "You never talk about her."

"I sometimes talk to my dad about her, but I don't really talk to everybody about her because I've learned that sometimes it makes it harder for me when I tell too many people," Flaco replied.

"Tell them what?" Ivy asked.

"My mom died when I was five years old," Flaco told her.

"Oh, Flaco!" Ivy gasped. "I didn't realize! I'm so sorry. You must think I am being a big baby because I'm so upset about my parents being separated."

"Not at all," he said. "I understand. What happened in my family doesn't make what you are experiencing easier. I know how strange it feels when everything you once knew changes.

"I was sad and angry all the time when my mom died. My family and school counselor helped me a lot. I made a box with some pictures and a letter mi madre wrote me that I keep by my bed. It helps me feel close to her when I feel sad and miss her. Although your parents are still here, you are going through the same type of feelings of loss because your life has changed from what you knew."

"So, what did you do to get over it?" Ivy asked.

"That's just it," said Flaco. "People think you are supposed to 'get over it,' but you don't you just learn to live with your new 'normal.' It's gotten better with time, but I realize that I don't want to 'get over it,' because I never want to forget my mom. The important thing to remember is that you don't have to heal on anybody's schedule, not even your own. My counselor called it the 'grieving process.' She explained why I was having so many different feelings all at once."

"Yeah, sometimes I can't tell if I'm angry or just sad, or both," Ivy realized.

"It can help to talk to an adult who knows about the grieving process so you can learn how to move through your feelings and not be stuck," Flaco assured her.

"Wow, Flaco, you really seem to know a lot about this," Ivy remarked.

"Well, it has been five years now, so I've had time to work through some of my sadness. It still comes up, like on my birthday and holidays," Flaco answered.

"I don't think I'll ever get used to this, though," Ivy lamented. "It's just so unfair."

"You might surprise yourself, Ivy," Flaco said. "Besides, in a way, you have more because you have two homes now."

"That's what Lyric said," replied Ivy.

"It's true," Flaco said. "Just talk to your mom. I'm sure it's not easy for her or your dad. They didn't want things to turn out this way for your family either. Besides, Ivy, you have all of us. We're all here for you. I'm really glad my dad moved us here, because having you kids as friends really helps me know that my life is still great, and that's what my mom would have wanted for me.

"My life is different than it was before," Flaco continued. "My abuelita says there is a cycle of life and death in everything, even the stars. She always tells me life is a mystery in many ways. You never know what is going to happen, exactly, so it's good to appreciate what you have."

"Wow, Flaco, that's deep," Ivy said. "Your abuelita sounds like the tribal elders. I think that's what they would tell me."

"Yeah," Flaco responded. "I think it's the same feelings people might go through with any kind of loss."

"Hey, Flaco," said Ivy. "I just was thinking, maybe I should go meet with the tribal elders that are near my dad's house. My dad always talks about the sweat lodge where he goes when he is struggling with something and wants to commune with the ancestors. I was never really interested before. I guess I always just expected my parents to have the answers I needed. I realize that adults don't always know what to do, either. It's OK to ask for help. I'm going to ask him to take me to one."

"Oh my gosh, Ivy, that sounds awesome. You should definitely do that!" Flaco responded excitedly.

"I should," Ivy agreed. "You know what would be fun? If all of our crew go to one of the powwows there—then I could show everyone the Fancy Dancing competitions."

"Yeah!" said Flaco. "That's a great idea. I think making some plans of your own is just what you need, instead of just wondering what's going to happen next."

Ivy wrapped her arms around Flaco and gave him the biggest hug!

"Thank you so much, Flaco, you really helped me

see things differently! I can't wait to tell my mom!" Ivy exclaimed.

Then she turned and ran towards home.

"Sure thing, Ivy!" Flaco shouted back and waved.

He smiled to himself and realized how much he had been through these past few years, and how good it felt to be able to turn his painful experience into something positive for his friend. As he turned and walked toward downtown to catch up with the crew, he could hear Ivy calling her mom.

"Mom! MOM!" Ivy shouted from the front garden as she ran up the walkway.

"Ivy, what is it, what's wrong?" Mom asked as she opened the door.

Ivy flung her arms around her mom as she began to tell her everything, all her plans, starting with inviting her friends to a local powwow, and how she wanted to take a trip for fall feast to visit her dad and grandmother. Ivy was out of breath, she was talking so fast.

"Whoa, slow down, kiddo, so I can hear everything you are saying," Mom said. "And Ivy, remember to take a mindful breath! Shall we go inside and call your dad? He will be so excited to hear all of your ideas! It is so good to see you so excited again!"

As Mom sighed with relief, Ivy came running past her again, stuffing a cookie in her mouth. "Bye, Mom, see ya later!"

"Wait, what?" asked Mom, a bit confused. "Where are you going?"

"Oh," Ivy paused, "I'm going to meet my friends at the thrift store. I want to tell them my plans!"

"I thought you wanted to call Dad," said Mom.

"I do! Can we call a little later?" Ivy replied. "Besides, everyone is waiting for me so we can go trick-or-treating!"

"Um, OK, honey, I'll see you later. Have fun! I love you!" said Mom.

When Ivy arrived at the store, her friends were just coming out. Belle saw her first.

"Ivy, you're back!" said Belle. "I'm so glad!"

"Yeah, Ivy, you're just in time," said V-Girl. "Look, we got you a cool hat."

"That *is* a cool hat," remarked Ivy. "Hey, can I tell you all something?"

"Sure," answered V-Girl. "You seemed upset when you left earlier. Is everything OK?"

"Well, I mean, everything is not really OK, but I think it will be."

So Ivy began to tell them everything that had been going on for her, and why she had been so sad and distant lately. She also told them she had a plan for a great adventure and wanted all of them to go with her.

Then she said, "I just want you all to know how much I appreciate having each of you in my life. I realize that holding my feelings inside was just hurting me more, and if I'm going to work through my feelings, I should talk about them with the people that care about me. Thank you so much, Flaco, for helping me understand that, and you too, Lyric. I plan to have many more talks with my mom and my dad about how this separation makes me feel. I still miss my dad, but I am able to look at it differently now. I get to spend time with both my mom and my dad, plus I have all of you."

"We all love you, Ivy," said V-Girl.

Everyone nodded in agreement with V-Girl.

The Kidz decided to stop by Gio's for one of his veggie special pizzas. The air was crisp, the birds were chirping, and the garden smelled of rosemary, sage, and lavender. Ivy looked around at her friends as they laughed and ate, and thought, *I am a really lucky kid*! *I have so much to be grateful for*!

CLASSIC
CAR SHOW

"BEAUTY AND THE BEAST"

Mural by Dante Orpilla, Dragon School

5
The Gift of Giving

"Lyric! LYRIC! Time to get up and get ready for school," Dad called out.

"I'm up. I'm up," Lyric insisted, as he got dressed and headed downstairs. "Come on down, your breakfast is ready," said Dad.

"Whoa, Dad, you made blueberry pancakes?!" Lyric marveled.

"Sure did. I thought we could have breakfast together, since I won't be here tomorrow," Dad added.

"What?! Where are you going?" asked Lyric.

"I am speaking at a conference this weekend," Dad replied. "I'll be going to the airport right after work."

“Dad, no! Did you forget about the Poetry Slam I’m competing in tonight?” cried Lyric.

“Oh, wait, is that today? I thought Mom said it was next weekend,” said Dad. “There’s just no way I can make it, Lyric. My flight leaves at 6 o’clock.”

“But Dad, you missed the last two and tonight’s the semifinals!” Lyric protested.

”Aww man! I’m really sorry, Lyric,” Dad apologized. “Maybe I . . . ”

“Yeah, OK Dad, I have to go now, so I’m not late,” Lyric sighed.

“What about your pancakes?” asked Dad.

“I’m not feeling very hungry. I’ll see you later,” said Lyric.

Disappointed, Lyric grabbed his backpack and headed out the door. He stopped by Flaco’s house, so they could walk to school together. Flaco was already coming down the steps when he got there.

“Hey, man, what’s up?” Flaco greeted his friend.

“Hey, bro,” Lyric murmured.

"Dude, why the long face? It's Friday!" chided an exuberant Flaco. "You look more like a Monday face."

"Yeah, whatever," said Lyric sadly. "My dad is going to miss my spoken word competition tonight. I really wanted him to come."

"Oh wow, no wonder you're upset," Flaco said. "Your mom is still coming though, right?"

"Yeah, she's coming," answered Lyric. "I just thought my dad would be there too."

"Mira! Flaco!" Flaco's dad called after him. "You're forgetting your lunch bag!"

"Yikes!" laughed Flaco. "That would have been a disaster, thanks Dad!"

"No problem, mijo. I can't have my boy passing out from not eating for two whole hours!" teased Mr. Medina. "Hi, Lyric! Buenos dias!"

"Good morning, Mr. Medina," Lyric responded.

"Flaco, did you ask Lyric if he wants to join us?" asked Mr. Medina.

"Not yet Dad, but we have to go or we'll be late for school," answered Flaco.

"OK, see you boys later. Have a great day!" Flaco's dad said, as he went back in the house.

So the two friends headed to school.

"Hey, what was your dad talking about?" asked Lyric.

"Huh? Oh yeah, you know how every November he serves a big dinner for everyone down at the shelter," answered Flaco. "Well, this year he's organizing a big dinner to serve at one of the encampments in the city."

"What, to the what, to the what-what?" Lyric quipped.

"The encampments, you know, curbside communities where the homeless have all those tents set up," answered Flaco.

"Um, no, I have no idea what you're talking about," Lyric confessed.

"What? You're kidding, right?" Flaco asked in disbelief.

"No, I'm not. Where are you talking about?" Lyric asked.

"Down on the West End, near the Ports," Flaco explained.

"Oh, I've never been over there. My parents say it's

a really bad area," said Lyric.

"Well no, it's not great. I don't go over there either, unless I'm with my dad. You don't think those people live over there because they want to, do you? They just really don't have any options," Flaco continued. "I think you really should come with us, actually. It just might be good for you."

"Good for me, how?" wondered Lyric.

"You'll see. Anyway, my dad wanted me to tell everyone about it, and you can let your parents know, also. We're meeting at Gio's this weekend so people can sign up for different volunteer positions. Gio is going to let us use his kitchen to cook all the food next week," Flaco explained.

By now the boys were in front of their school and the first bell was ringing. "Hey, there's the bell," Flaco said. "We'll talk more later."

Just then Ivy skipped up.

"Hi, Lyric. Hi, Flaco. Was that the first or second bell that just rang?" asked Ivy.

"First," Flaco and Lyric chimed in unison.

Ivy continued excitedly, "I have great news I want to talk to you all about. Let's meet in the school garden at first recess. Oh, and if you see the twins before I do, tell them to come too!"

"Sure thing, Ivy. Can you at least give us a hint?" Flaco asked impatiently.

Ivy broke out into some Fancy Dancing and a Navajo song as she moved toward her class line-up, with a sly grin.

Flaco and Lyric looked at each other and blurted out, "Powwow!" at the same time as they slapped high fives.

"Oh man, I wonder if it is?" queried Flaco.

Just then Pixel came sliding into line. He was last in line and knelt down to tie his shoe with his headphones around his neck and his hair sticking up.

"Wonder if it is what?!" he asked

"A powwow," repeated Flaco. "Ivy said she has a surprise for us, and we're hoping it's a powwow!"

"Cool!" sang Pixel. "She said something about that the other day. Do you know if it is OK to record the songs there? I would love to have some for my music library."

"I'm pretty sure you need to ask permission first," Flaco advised. "It's about respect."

"Oh, yeah, for sure," Pixel agreed.

The Kidz stood in line to hear the morning announcements from the Principal and to take a mindful breath.

Belle's teacher led the school in morning meditation. "Breathe in 1-2-3, and breathe out 3-2-1."

"Everyone have a friendly Friday," encouraged the principal, as everyone headed to class.

When the recess bell finally rang, the Kidz each headed for the school garden. The garden was where Ms. Portal taught the Konscious Kidz and their classmates about all kinds of amazing things: eco-warriors, food justice, planting, and growing vegetables.

Everyone loved the garden, and everyone loved Ms. Portal, their garden teacher. She was always so kind and helpful.

Ms. Portal was clearing fall leaves when the kids burst in through the open gate.

"Hello, everyone. What are you all up to?" she asked.

"Oh hello, Ms Portal," Ivy exclaimed. "I have some exciting news I want to share with everyone, so I'm happy that you're here."

"What is it, Ivy?" urged Belle.

"I am inviting all of you, my best friends, and you too, Ms. Portal, to attend a powwow not far from here," announced Ivy excitedly.

"Thank you, Ivy. That will be quite an honor," Ms. Portal replied.

"That sounds awesome, Ivy. We were wondering if that was your surprise," said Flaco. "There's something I want everyone to know about, also."

"Hey, Flaco, hang on, where's Lyric?" Pixel interrupted.

The kids were all so excited that they didn't notice one of them was missing! They began to look around and call out for Lyric.

"LYRIC!"

Just then Lyric emerged from behind the peach tree.

"I was just sitting under the tree. What's all the excitement about?" asked Lyric.

"Hey, man, Ivy invited us all to a powwow when her dad comes to town for the holiday! I was just about to tell everyone what I mentioned to you this morning, about my dad organizing a big dinner for one of the homeless encampments next Wednesday," Flaco replied. "Don't forget to tell your parents—we need all the help we can get."

"That sounds awesome," said V-Girl. "Belle and I were talking about wanting to do something for the homeless just yesterday."

"Yeah, V-Girl, and don't forget Grandma is coming from Denver next week to visit. I know she'll want to help 'cause she's always teaching us about helping others," said Belle.

"Hey, I have a good idea," Pixel chimed in. "What if we also do a collection in the neighborhood, for warm blankets and sleeping bags?"

"That's a great idea," Flaco agreed. "It is getting cold at night, and I'm sure there are people that could really use those kinds of things. While we're at it, let's try to get people to donate socks and warm coats or jackets too."

"I know, we'll do a Winter Warm Up Drive and put together winter care packages for those in need," added Pixel.

"Yeah," said Belle, "this is exciting! Let's make a list of things, and people can choose what they can donate."

"Right, but we need to make it as easy as possible for people to give to our cause. What if we go door to door with the list first and then go back and pick up stuff the next day?" Lyric suggested.

"Maybe we can get some of our parents to drive us around town, so we have a way to carry all of the great things people are going to donate," gushed V-Girl. "I just know this is going to be big!"

For the next couple of days the Kidz went around and collected donations. By the time Tuesday came, they had a good assortment of items from the list.

The next day they all met at Flaco's house to load up the donations, food, and serving supplies, before boarding Mr. Medina's Food Justice Bus and heading across town, to one of the largest encampments.

Once they arrived, Mr. Medina began setting up tables with the volunteers, to prepare to serve food.

While that was happening, the Kidz and several parents began handing out all of the donated items to whoever needed them.

"This has got to be so hard to live like this," Lyric thought to himself.

As people began to line up for dinner, he noticed that everyone seemed to be in pretty good spirits.

"I don't get it," Lyric said to Mr. Medina.

"What is it you don't get?" Mr. Medina asked.

"Well," Lyric began. "I can't even imagine how difficult it must be to live like this. Yet so many of the people here today seem to have such positive attitudes. I think I would be devastated and crying, like all of the time, if I had to live here."

"I'm sure everyone here has had moments of despair," began Mr. Medina. "I'm sure many have found themselves in tears. However, having someone, or in today's case, many people, show you a little love and compassion restores a person's hope in humanity. That is what we really want to do today, Lyric. Besides just giving them things like food and supplies, which they absolutely need, we want to offer them hope. Hope is a very powerful thing, Lyric. You never know how strong you are until you need to be."

"I'm just really lucky my folks are able to have a house for us to live in," Lyric reflected.

"You want to know a little secret, Lyric?" Mr. Medina shared.

"Sure, what is it?" asked Lyric.

"Coming here and being of

service to the community doesn't just help them, it helps me," confessed Mr. Medina.

"Huh? How so?" Lyric puzzled.

"It reminds me to be humble and grateful," Mr. Medina explained. "It reminds me to focus on the good in my life and not what I may feel that I am missing."

"Yeah, I'm feeling that way right now," Lyric realized.

"Now let's get this food served, because I see some hungry faces. I'm sure they'll appreciate this food a lot more once it's on their plate and they can eat it," urged Mr. Medina.

So they spent the next few hours serving food and talking to the people in the encampment about all sorts of topics. At the end of the day Lyric knew why Flaco had wanted him to come. He went to his friend and thanked him.

"Hey, Flaco, I saw how much these people were grateful for our help. What I'm not sure of is whether coming here helped them more than it helped me. I guess you knew that, huh?" Lyric acknowledged.

"Yup!" said Flaco, and they threw their arms around each other as they got back on the Food Justice bus to head home.

DISCUSSION QUESTIONS TO REVIEW AFTER EACH STORY

1) What character or situation do you most relate to in this story? Why?

2) If you were in this story, is there anything you would do differently to solve the challenges the characters faced?

3) In this story, can you find where a character used one or more of the following principles: compassion, empathy, forgiveness, inclusion, gratitude, mindfulness, patience, kindness, listening, courage, love, honesty. Which character? What did they do?

4) Which character would you like to have as a friend and why?

5) This story has made me reconsider or think twice about . . . because . . .

6) Which part of this story caused the strongest feelings for you? What were the feelings?

7) Describe an example of a character being grateful. How do you practice gratitude in your life?

8) Why do you think the authors chose to write this story?

Visit www.konsciouskidz.com for additional resources.

MURALS IN ORDER OF APPEARANCE

ANGEL DE LA GUARDA (GUARDIAN ANGEL) - CHRIS GRANILLO

1721 International Blvd. (behind Jalisco restaurant), East Oakland, CA

As a Palm Springs native and current Oakland resident, Chris Granillo is the epitome of what it means to be an artist. Having grown up in the desert, he never let a lack of opportunities or resources dictate his ability to be and grow as an artist. Chris has used his talent to uplift, unify, and beautify communities and has created outdoor art galleries that neighborhoods are proud to call their own.

BORN TO BE LOVED - CHRIS "ROYYAL DOG" SHIM

1128 Lincoln Ave, Alameda, CA

Graffiti artist Royyal Dog uses his work to conceptually bridge the gap between cultures and traditional limitations. Originally from Seoul, South Korea, Chris has created magnificently beautiful works in Los Angeles, San Francisco, New York, Guam, Hawaii, Isreal, Korea, Amsterdam, and more. His depictions of girls and women of color in traditional Korean Hanboks are as revolutionary as they are breathtaking.

LOVE YOUR CITY - FREE HUMANITY

1000 Central Avenue, Alameda, CA

Free Humanity is an L.A.-based Street Artist/Muralist, internationally known for his multicultural hearts and positive message. His mission statement sums up his ideal for his work: "Taking back the humanity stolen from our minds by social manipulation and planting seeds of positivity through art and consciousness."

THE RED ROAD - INTERTRIBAL FRIENDSHIP HOUSE/JASON DOBBS

523 International Blvd., Oakland, CA

"We envision a future where Native people in the Bay Area are rooted in strong cultural connections, intergenerational healing and traditions that will help future generations."—Carol Wahpepoh IFH Executive Director

BEAUTY AND THE BEAST - DRAGON SCHOOL/DANTE ORPILLA

10th Avenue & Madison St., Oakland, CA

Dragon School, in Chinatown, Oakland, enlisted Dante Orpilla to create this piece. During a difficult time in his life, Dante discovered art as a therapeutic way to transcend his circumstances. His work as an artist is aligned with Dragon School's mission to unite and beautify communities through art.

ACKNOWLEDGMENTS AND GRATITUDE

This endeavor was truly a labor of love and the fruit of individuals from overlapping communities generously sharing their time, talents, and resources with us.

The ever-growing list of those we are humbly grateful to follows (but isn't limited to the below): Our daughters Simone and Vivienne for inspiration and content contributions. Our team: Jerl Laws, Illustrator; Barbara Genetin, Book Designer; Amaya Edwards, Photographer; Yolanda Cázares, Publishing Mentor and Advisor; Clair Dunne, Research and Business Administrator. Editing and feedback: Cecilia Santini, Gabrielle Hoffman-Ellis, Janine Connor, Huyen "Kiki" Vo, Maria Yen, and Irma George. Business Coaching and Mentorship: Lisa Lucheta and Naomi Tyler. Also much gratitude to Richard Vance, Kate Schatz, Richard Vaterlaus, Linda Buran, and Dylan Reedy. We the authors wish to express deep admiration to the multi-talented Barbara Genetin whose knowledge and experience took us beyond.

Street Art/Muralists: Chris Granillo, Chris "Royyal Dog" Shim, Free Humanity, Dante Orpilla/Dragon School Oakland, Intertribal Friendship House.

We must give a special thank you to our Kickstarter backers who made this project possible by believing in not only what the project is, but why this project is important. Every single one of you was critically instrumental in this endeavor coming to fruition. We could not have accomplished this without you.

Now, our greatest hope is that what we have created for you and the children of the world fulfills your expectation of us and serves the children and their caregivers, in a way that enriches their lives and elevates our global community.

THANK YOU